First published 1989
Reprinted 1990
Second edition published 1991
by The Lost Forests Pty Ltd.

Copyright © The Lost Forests Pty Ltd.
265 Burke Road, Glen Iris 3146
Melbourne, Victoria, Australia
Telephone (03) 885 9716. Facsimile (03) 885 3143

Original Lost Forests concept, characters and storyline created by Tony Barber.

National Library of Australia
cataloguing in publication data

Barber, Anthony.
        The Lost Forests.
        ISBN 0 646 06871 7
        I. Cory, Rowena. II. Johnston, Chris. III. Title.
A823.3

Printed by Vega Press Pty Ltd
91 Railway Road Blackburn Victoria 3130, Australia
Telephone (03) 878 2222 Facsimile (03) 894 1039
Printed in Australia

THE LOST FORESTS

Written by Tony Barber and Rowena Cory

Illustrated by Rowena Cory and Chris Johnston

Ever since his parents had died in 1874, Timothy Barber had walked the length and breadth of England with his Uncle Fumble Fingers Farrow, a carnival juggler.

It was Timothy's job to clean and repair the juggling equipment and to make sure his Uncle was on time for each performance.

One afternoon, upon entering a seaside town, Uncle Fumble Fingers grabbed Timothy by the ear and said: "Now listen boy. I'm going to have my afternoon snooze. Wake me when the town clock strikes seven. And this time, no excuses like losing your way in a forest, or stopping to watch leaves fall.

Now, be off with you!"

Timothy rubbed his ear resentfully. *He* was the one who did all the work. Uncle Fumble Fingers hadn't even offered to teach him how to juggle. Not that it would be of any use, as his Uncle was a terrible juggler.

It just wasn't fair!

As Timothy walked out of the town, he decided to forget his troubles – at least until seven o'clock. Until then he was free to enjoy the nearby forest. Suddenly he stood still.
This forest was somehow different.

Was it the way the light filtered through the leaves? Was it the forest noises, strange half-heard teasing whispers?
Could these trees be *watching* him?
Then he heard it, a faint but frantic squeal.

With his heart in his mouth, Timothy looked up and saw a pig. It was entangled in the branches of a tree. This was not so unusual except it was caught by one of its wings! As it tried to wriggle free, it squealed pitifully.

"I've never seen a pig with wings before," Timothy exclaimed.

"And you wouldn't have seen *me* if I hadn't been trapped," snapped the little creature.

Timothy's jaw dropped.

"Well, don't just stand there staring, help me," pleaded the pig.

"I'm very sorry," Timothy said, as he climbed up and strained to free him. "It's just that … you've got wings!"

The pig grunted, wriggled free and dropped into Timothy's arms: "If you knew anything about the history of Pigmiedom, you'd know that we all had enormous wings once and our tails were straight from the slipstream of flying. But gradually most pigs' wings got smaller and smaller, till they evolved away. All except we Pigmies. The last True Flying Pigs."

"But why haven't I seen …?" Timothy began.
"You don't think we let just anyone into our world?"
the Pigmie snorted. Timothy was sure the
surrounding trees sniggered. "No, only 'special'
Big Folk can visit Pigmie Valley. After all, we
don't want every local busybody dropping in
unannounced!"
Timothy shuffled his feet. "Do you think I could
visit?" he asked shyly.

The Pigmie settled importantly on the forest floor,
too intent on his lecture to answer.
"Where do you think we mythical creatures come
from, anyway? We're from the Other Worlds,
of course.
Only we aren't mythical, we're real. Lots of us,
including some you've never seen before,
retreated through the trapdoors as you Big
Folk spread all over the world."

"Oh," Timothy mumbled. How could he ask to see the Pigmie's home after that?

The soft sniggering and chittering of the surrounding forest seemed to mock him.

"Don't you want to see Pigmie Valley?" demanded the Pigmie.

"Oh yes please. I'd love to. But how …?"

"Through a trapdoor, of course," the Pigmie snapped. "You're sitting on one!"

Timothy was certain he heard the surrounding trees snigger again. He rolled to his feet and, sure enough, he'd been sitting on what was unmistakably a trapdoor, complete with a round metal handle.

He could have sworn it wasn't there before. The Pigmie threw the trapdoor open, flooding the clearing with a glowing shaft of light that danced over the faces of the encircling trees. A rush of giggling noises greeted Timothy, who thought he could also hear the sound of running water.

"Well?" the Pigmie prompted. "What are you waiting for?"

Timothy swallowed, his heart racing.

Just as he was about to take the first step down-wards, Timothy heard something that made his heart sink. Faintly and persistently, above the chittering lure of the Other Worlds, came the sound of the town clock striking the hour.

"Oh no," he gasped. "Six … seven … eight." Reluctantly, he looked up from the sea of swirl-ing light, across to the hovering Pigmie.

"I can't come with you. I forgot, you see." Timothy took a step back. "My Uncle Fumble Fingers will be furious …"

"You're not going, are you?" the Pigmie asked.

"I have to. I'm sorry …"

"But I didn't have a chance to thank you, or … or anything," the little Pigmie insisted. "Wait." He unhooked a small cloth bag from the under-side of the trapdoor.

"Here." The Pigmie gave it to Timothy.

"I … I didn't mean to be rude. I was just so frightened. Big Folk aren't always kind to Pigmies. But you, you're special. Keep this seed bag and remember – wherever you go, listen for the sounds you're hearing now. And when you hear them, plant the seeds. When these trees appear, so will another trapdoor.

"But be warned. While anyone can enter our hidden world, not everyone can leave.
There are some who would do us harm.
Those we change for the better. So be careful who you tell."
"Oh I wouldn't. But what do you mean, change?" Timothy whispered.
The Pigmie glanced at the surrounding trees.
"The unbelievers become our Guardian Trees.

They must protect us for evermore."
Timothy couldn't help grinning.
"So be careful," the Pigmie cried out as he circled, sinking into the shaft of light. "And don't forget …"
"I won't, not ever." Timothy called back.
Then he turned on his heels and ran. When he glanced back over his shoulder, the circle of trees was quite dark. He had only the moon to guide him back to town.

Timothy's heart was pounding madly as he looked for his Uncle. But it was Fumble Fingers Farrow who found Timothy first.

A heavy hand clamped down onto Timothy's shoulder.

"Ungrateful wretch. Useless boy," his Uncle roared. "Can't trust you to do anything right …"

As he took a swing at Timothy, Uncle Fumble Fingers nearly fell down some steps.

Instinctively, Timothy ducked and ran off.

"Come back here, you … you …"

But Timothy didn't stay to hear any more.

He ran down the cobbled street to the docks, his Uncle staggering behind him.

With no time to think, Timothy saw a large wooden chest among a pile of luggage, which was being loaded onto a sailing ship. Before his Uncle came around the corner, Timothy climbed in, closing the lid behind him. Seconds later, there was a clunking noise. The chest lurched to one side and Timothy felt himself rise.

He pushed against the lid, but the catch had locked, trapping him inside.

Clutching the bag of seeds, he wished he'd taken the Pigmie's offer, but regrets were useless.

Some time later, Timothy felt very tired and was soon asleep, disturbed only by the rumbling of his empty stomach and the sway of the ship at sea.

Much later, he was woken by the sound of creaking hinges as the chest was opened. For a moment he couldn't remember where he was, then he was blinded by a flood of lamplight. A girl shrieked. A deep voice boomed.
"Stand back Miss Rosebud." A huge hand lifted Timothy by the arm. "I'll deal with this stowaway."

Blinking furiously, Timothy made out the shape of a little girl in the light of the lamp.
"But I'm not …" he began, trying to keep his balance as the steward dragged him through the luggage hold. "I'm not a stowaway. I was running away from my Uncle.
He was going to beat me!"

Timothy stopped resisting and let the steward drag him up on deck. Not only was he thought to be a criminal, but also he'd lost the bag of seeds. Feeling utterly miserable, Timothy didn't even look up as someone asked: "Is this the stowaway?"

"Yes sir," the steward replied. "He was hidden in your Miss Rosebud's trunk."

"Is this true?" the little girl's father asked. His gentle tone of voice made Timothy look up hopefully. Maybe he would under-stand.

"I wasn't stowing away, sir. My Uncle was going to beat me again. I hid, then the lid wouldn't open and …"

"Show me your back," the man said.

Timothy turned around and lifted his shirt.

The two men gasped. "You can't treat this boy like a common stowaway," Rosebud's father insisted.

"Captain won't turn the ship around and take him back, sir. There's his passage to pay as well …"

"I'll see to that." The father smiled at Timothy. "He can be … a companion for my little Rosebud."

"I can't pay you," Timothy said. Rosebud's father studied him. "We have a sheep farm in Australia. You can pay me back with work."

And so Timothy sailed to Australia and grew up on Rosebud's farm. As the years passed, Uncle Fumble Fingers became an unpleasant but distant memory and the Pigmie and his bag of seeds became a wonderful dream.

As young adults will, Timothy and Rosebud fell in love and then married. Determined to make a life for himself and Rosebud, Timothy packed their bags and together they set off around Australia, travelling from country fair to small town fete.

Here Timothy would demonstrate his amazing skills of body-painting.

He would paint the skin showing through the holes in poor people's clothes to exactly match the material that was torn. This saved them the cost of replacing worn shirts, pants and dresses.

Such was his fame that people came from all around. Rich people even tore holes in their best clothing just so they could show their friends Timothy's body-painting.

Timothy and Rosebud were successful,
very successful.
So much so that they decided to buy a
travelling van.
Rosebud was unpacking an old wooden
chest when she discovered an old cloth bag.
She asked Timothy:
"Do you want this or will I throw it out?"
"What?" Timothy replied. "By crikey!

It's the seeds of the Guardian Trees …"
"Guardian Trees?" Rosebud repeated.
Timothy grinned, "Do you remember how I hid
from my Uncle in that very chest?" he asked.
Rosebud nodded.
Timothy told her of his meeting with the Pigmie.
Rosebud then agreed that they should find one
of the special places where the sounds of the
Other Worlds could be heard.

Late one evening after months of searching they finally discovered a special place. Timothy planted a seed there, and he and Rosebud retired for the night.

The following morning, as they neared this special place, Timothy whispered,
"Rosebud, you mustn't be too disappointed. It was such a long time ago, maybe the seeds won't work."

"Oh look," she gasped. "The trees have faces…"

"Faces," Timothy repeated, feeling twelve years old again. He felt as if he might see the Pigmie caught in the tree if he looked up. And there in the centre of the forest was a trapdoor.

Rosebud and Timothy's eyes met.

They took a deep breath and opened it up. A flood of sparkling light filled the early morning, dancing around the encircling trees. The sniggering, giggling voices and sounds were enticing them to enter the Other Worlds. Timothy and Rosebud held hands, smiled at each other and stepped downwards.

Rosebud gasped in amazement at what she saw!
"Oh my goodness. Look, pink and yellow trees."
"And look over there," said Timothy.
"Oh, oh … watch out!"
He fell to one side, pulling Rosebud with him,
as a green, speeding wheel whizzed
past them.

"What was that?" Rosebud exclaimed.
"I don't know," answered Timothy, "but something
was sitting in the centre of it!"
As they stood up, Rosebud noticed many pathways.
"We must be at some kind of junction that leads
to different parts of the Other Worlds," Timothy said.
"I wonder where Pigmie Valley could be?"

"Look out," Rosebud cried, pointing behind her. Timothy spun around to see a black and white cat about to fall from a nearby tree branch. Throwing himself forward, Timothy lunged under the plunging cat to break its fall. They both tumbled over the edge of a creek bank into the shallow, sun-dappled water.

As Rosebud struggled through the ferns after them, she heard a chorus of different giggles, but her concern was for Timothy and the cat.

She found them, sitting in the creek bed, both drenched. Above the gentle sound of running water the giggling grew louder.

"It's those Gigalot Possums," the cat explained resignedly. "They think it's hilarious when one of us trips over. I'm a Catastrophe Cat, you see."

"Well hello! Timothy and Rosebud at your service," Timothy smiled. "I was really looking for a little Pigmie friend of mine. Do you know …?"

"Here they come now," Catastrophe Cat said. "They're always around when something interesting happens!"

Timothy passed the dripping cat to Rosebud, who dried him off and wrapped his cut paw.

As Timothy climbed out of the creek, he was met by a fleet of flying pink pigs.

"Pigmies halt!" cried the Captain of the Pigmie
Flying Fleet.

The Pigmies hovered behind him as he circled
closer to observe Timothy and Rosebud.

"Explain yourselves!" he ordered.

"I don't think he's the Pigmie you met," Rosebud
whispered.

Timothy took the bag of seeds from his pocket
and was about to retell his story when the
Catastrophe Cat intervened.

"Look, he has the seeds. He knows all about us.
And he saved me from a nasty fall."

In the branches above their heads was a whole
family of Gigalot Possums. They hung by their
tails and gave out a chorus of cheeky giggles.

Rosebud looked up and gasped.

"She's nice," whispered a shy baby possum.

"Who asked you?" demanded the Pigmie Captain.

The baby giggled nervously.

"Oh you sweet thing," said Rosebud.

Then a crowd of Nice Mice appeared. The fattest one jumped up onto a mushroom and declared:

"This calls for a celebration!"

Other mice took up the cry.

"A party!"

"Lots to eat …"

"As long as it's not cheese!"

"You lot would use any excuse for a party," snorted the Pigmie Captain.

"Who needs an excuse?" smirked the fattest of the Nice Mice.

The Pigmie Captain ignored him.

"All right Pigmies," he ordered, "escort these Big Folk to Pigmie Valley …"

"Wait!" cried a yellow grub, who was as big as a cat. Rosebud gasped. "It's one of those Fidgety Grubs," explained Catastrophe Cat, who had taken a liking to Rosebud.

"Didgety Ridge is the best place for a party,"
the Fidgety Grub insisted. "Lots of yummy
things to eat in our pink and yellow trees … "
"Oh oh," cried an Oh Oh, who had just rolled
into the clearing inside his Whiz Wheel.
"Let's not argue. Let's celebrate … Oh oh!"
Down swooped the Pigmie Captain.
"Exactly, and Pigmie Valley is the place to
have it."
"What about Puggle Town?" piped up a
small voice.
Timothy and Rosebud looked down to see
a plump little pink Puggle.
"We've ever so many nice things there …"
A whole chorus of Gigalot Possums descended
from the trees, as well as a flotilla of Fidgcty
Grubs, a party-sized serve of Nice Mice and at
least a dozen Catastrophes waiting to happen.
They surrounded Timothy and Rosebud,
touching their hair and clothing, offering them
food and drink, and insisting that they come
back to their homes.
Timothy laughed, saying to Rosebud: "It feels
like we're already home!"

Much later, when even the Nice Mice had eaten enough and all that was left was crumbs, Timothy and Rosebud thanked their hosts.

"Oh, but you can't go," a little possum giggled.

"Yes they can," a Catastrophe Cat insisted.

"I say no," declared the fattest of the Nice Mice. "Anyone who's as nice as they are doesn't deserve to get turned into a Guardian Tree …"

"Tree?" Rosebud whispered to Timothy.

"These are good Big Folk. We can let them go back, but only on the condition that they don't tell any bad Big Folk about us …"

"Now hear this," announced the Pigmie Captain.

"Timothy and Rosebud are our official Big Folk Friends. Whenever they visit us, you are to make them welcome …"

"Pompous old busybody," smirked the fattest of the Nice Mice. "As if we wouldn't!"

"Hmmm." The Pigmie cleared his throat importantly.

"Oh, oh," cried an Oh Oh. "He's going to make a speech!"

Timothy and Rosebud giggled.

"We'd love to come back," she told them.

"And you can be sure," Timothy added, "that we won't give you away."

After saying goodbye to their new friends, Timothy and Rosebud returned to the world above. They continued travelling across the countryside, discovering trapdoors and enjoying many trips down to the Other Worlds.

Then Timothy took Rosebud back to her parents' sheep farm, where their son Arthur was born.

To support his young family, Timothy resumed his travelling life, sending the money he made from body-painting back to Rosebud.

As Arthur grew up, Rosebud told him all about the Other Worlds, but he had no desire at all to visit them. In fact, he refused to believe that they existed at all. When he was 21 years old, Arthur took over the running of the sheep farm and Rosebud joined Timothy on his travels.

Many times they invited Arthur to join them and see the Other Worlds, but he preferred to stay on the farm.

Then one day in 1932, Arthur was told that Timothy and Rosebud had disappeared. Search parties looked for them everywhere, but could find no trace of the travelling performers.

The many forests of talking Guardian Trees also disappeared and with them the magic trapdoors. Arthur realised that his parents had decided to stay in the Other Worlds forever, so he said nothing. He stored the few belongings they had left behind and went about his normal life.

Arthur knew he thought differently to his parents, and that they would all be happier if things were left just as they were.

Years later Arthur's own son, Tony, asked what had become of his grandparents.

Arthur had noticed an unwelcome tendency in his son to daydream and lose himself in fairy tales. To his way of thinking, Tony just wasn't taking life seriously enough.

When the boy asked, 'Where did granny and grandad go?', Arthur replied, 'They went on a long voyage. Always on the move. Just couldn't settle down'.

"Didn't you want to go with them?"
Tony asked.

"Certainly not. Them and their crazy talk of magic trapdoors and flying pigs ..."

"Flying pigs?" Tony asked.

Arthur realised he'd said a bit too much:

"Guardian Trees! Nothing in it. Lot of nonsense."
He leant closer to Tony.

"Listen, boy, you apply yourself to your studies. Take up something sensible. Make something of yourself."

But try as he might, Tony didn't seem to fit in with any of the things his father wanted him to do. Finally, as a young man, Tony left home to travel around Australia like his grandfather before him.

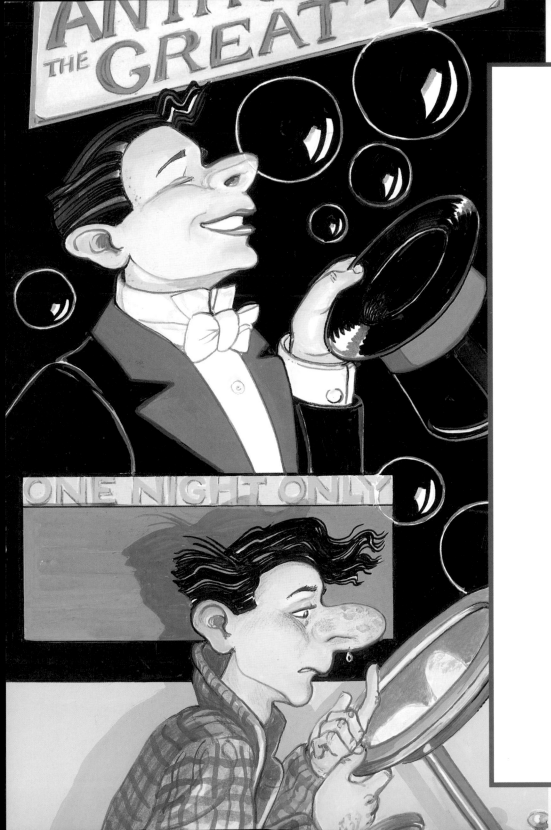

And just like his grandfather, Tony discovered he had an unusual talent – he could blow soap bubbles through his nose! Big ones, little ones, even double-headed bubbles. People came from near and far to see this phenomenon. Tony was a success, but it was hardly the sort of success that his father, Arthur, would have liked.

In his letters home, Tony was careful not to go into detail.

Even when he married, Tony sent his father only a brief note.

Then disaster struck. Tony developed an allergy to the new, scented soaps. His nose blew up to seven times its normal size and turned a sickening shade of green.

Forced to find another way of earning a living, Tony and his family went to America where he made soft, cuddly toys, finally achieving the kind of success that would have made his father proud.

Upon his father's death, Tony returned to Australia. It was while sorting through his father's belongings that he discovered his grandparents' things in the spare room.

Feeling just a little uneasy, though he couldn't think why, Tony swept the dust from an old chest. As he lifted the lid, Tony wondered what secrets he would learn of the mysterious grandparents he had never had a chance to meet.

In the bottom of the chest, tucked inside an old walking boot was a bag of seeds and a note addressed to Arthur.

Tony opened the note and read:

Dear Son,

Here is one last chance to join us.

Remember to listen for the sounds, plant a seed and wait. Your Mother and I hope to see you one day in the Other Worlds. We'll be much the same as we were last time we said goodbye, as time moves differently there.

Your Loving Father, Timothy

On the back of the note was a rough map of Australia giving the location of the special places.

"This must be something to do with the trapdoors that father mentioned," Tony mumured.

With the map in one hand and the bag of seeds in the other, Tony set off to locate the special places. But the bush was gone. Houses and shops stood where Timothy and Rosebud had once wandered down wooded paths.

Hoping that he would recognise the sounds, Tony tried not to despair. He could be seen in the middle of a busy road, one finger in his ear, the other ear pressed to the ground.

He even used a doctor's stethoscope.

Finally, one day, he heard the sounds just as he'd imagined they'd be, drifting from an empty shop. Tony borrowed the key from the landlord and went inside.

Sure enough, after he'd lifted the floor boards, the sounds were even louder. He planted a seed and, keeping his fingers crossed, waited for hours. Nothing happened.

Feeling utterly despondent, Tony returned the shop key.

All night he lay awake, thinking about his father's reluctance to tell him more about his grandparents and about how the bag and note had remained untouched for all those years. Unable to let it end like this, Tony was on the landlord's doorstep first thing in the morning. "You'd better make up your mind quickly," the landlord warned. "I have another person coming to see the shop at lunchtime."

Tony borrowed the key again and hurried away.

Maybe he was crazy, but he couldn't abandon Timothy and Rosebud without one last look. His heart was pounding madly as he turned the key in the door lock.

Tony couldn't see a thing through the dirty windows, so he wasn't prepared for the tall trunks of a forest. A wave of sniggering, chittering, teasing whispers greeted him.

A tree seemed to wink!

And there in the middle of the forest was a trapdoor. Tony grabbed the trapdoor handle and slowly lifted it up.

Dancing beams of light filled the air. A rush of mysterious sounds engulfed him.

Hardly daring to breathe, Tony stepped down into another world.

He was at a pretty, fern-filled crossroad. It seemed to be early morning here too, but he remembered what Grandfather Timothy had said about time moving differently.

A rustle of leaves told him that he wasn't alone. Tony looked up to see a little pink snout peeping through the foliage of a tree.

"Why, hello," Tony said, smiling. "What's a pig doing in a tree?"

The flying Pigmie sneezed.

"Hiding," she whispered shyly. "My mummy always told me to be careful of Big Folk. Only I've never seen one before …"

"Do you know of Timothy and Rosebud?" Tony asked. The little Pigmie said no.

Tony's heart sank.

"I've heard of them," a boy Pigmie announced eagerly, swooping down to land on a low branch. "But I thought they were only make-believe, to scare us into going to bed on time."

"Big Folk?" enquired an anxious voice from above. A portly mother Pigmie flew into the clearing. "Now children what have I told you … Eeeeeee!"

She swooped down to protect her baby Pigmies. "Shoo … Shoo! You … you big brute."

"But I'm not," Tony said, trying not to smile. "I'm looking for Timothy and Rosebud. Have you seen them?"

"No one has, not for a long time," she sniffed.

"Oh." Tony sank down to sit on a rock, sharing it with a Gigalot Possum. "I, I guess I'll just have to keep looking. Find the other trapdoors and … "

"All the trapdoors are closed," the mother Pigmie told him.

"We had to close them. Too many bad Big Folk wandered through …"

"Too much work turning them into Guardian Trees," admitted the fattest of two Nice Mice who had joined them.

Tony turned to the Pigmie mother for an explanation.

"Well", she said primly, "we couldn't let them go back."

"Back," Tony muttered. "I'd better get back or that landlord will …"

"You can't go yet," she told him. "There's so much to see."

"Wait till the other Gigalots hear about this!" said the Gigalot Possum.

"Oh no, he must come back to Pigmie Valley first," insisted the Pigmie mother. "No one will believe we've found a real Big Folk…"

"Oh oh," a nearby Oh Oh rolled his eyes.

"But I must go," Tony said, before there could be an argument "One of those bad Big Folk will close this trap door if I can't find a way to keep it open …"

"Please don't go." The baby Pigmie flew to land on his shoulder and nuzzle his neck. "I like you."

"But I have to go," Tony said, lifting her off his shoulder.

"It's up to me to keep this trapdoor open, or I'll never find Timothy and Rosebud …" Suddenly it came to him. "I know! I'll rent the shop myself. Then I'll hunt for other special places and open those trapdoors.

"But you can't! What if bad Big Folk start coming again?" demanded the mother Pigmie.

"I'll make sure they don't," Tony assured her. "I'll be your protector …"

"Does that mean you can come and see us?" whispered the little Pigmie eagerly.

Tony smiled fondly, saying: "I'd love to. But I'll have to pay the rent somehow."

He rubbed his jaw thoughtfully. The creatures adopted poses of deep thought.

"What's rent?" asked the baby Pigmie.

Tony grinned. "It's something too hard to explain …"

"Can we be friends?" asked the young Pigmie.
"Anyone would be proud to have you for… that's it!"
Tony stopped talking and looked around him.
"How would you like to be my models for soft,
cuddly toys? Then little children could take them
home… without disturbing you!"

"We'd love to," they all shouted.
"That way, I could afford to keep the shop open dur-
ing the day, while at night, I search the Other Worlds
for my grandparents. I'd better get started. I've got a
feeling that lots more friends and adventures will be
coming my way as I discover more Lost Forests."

The Lost Forests series of books and audio tapes

Discover Tony Barber's world of the hidden forests and the characters that dwell within in *The Lost Forests* series of books and audio tapes.

The Lost Forests
Meet fascinating creatures like Catastrophe Cats, Nice Mice, Fidgety Grubs, Gigalot Possums, and many more weird and wonderful animals.

Marco and The Book of Wisdom
Follow Marco Puggle as he struggles over the special Puggle Book of Wisdom with the mischievous Whiz Lid the Wizard and his helper Buggle Uggle.

Flying's Easy
S'Easy is a very special Puggle. He lives in an unusual looking house made from old musical instruments. S'Easy believes that everything in life will work out just fine!

Double Trouble
Big trouble in Puggle Town as Whiz Lid the Wizard causes more worries with his magic and spells. Meet Penelope, Primrose, S'Easy, Bo and Marco.